Disney · PIXAR
Treasury

This edition published by Parragon Books Ltd in 2014
Parragon Books Ltd
Chartist House
15–17 Trim Street
Bath BA1 1HA, UK
www.parragon.com

ISBN 978-1-4723-5009-1

Printed in China

Disney · PIXAR
Treasury

Bath · New York · Cologne · Melbourne · Delhi
Hong Kong · Shenzhen · Singapore · Amsterdam

This book belongs to

....

....

Contents

Monsters, Inc. 11

Monsters University 41

Finding Nemo 73

Toy Story 107

Toy Story 2 137

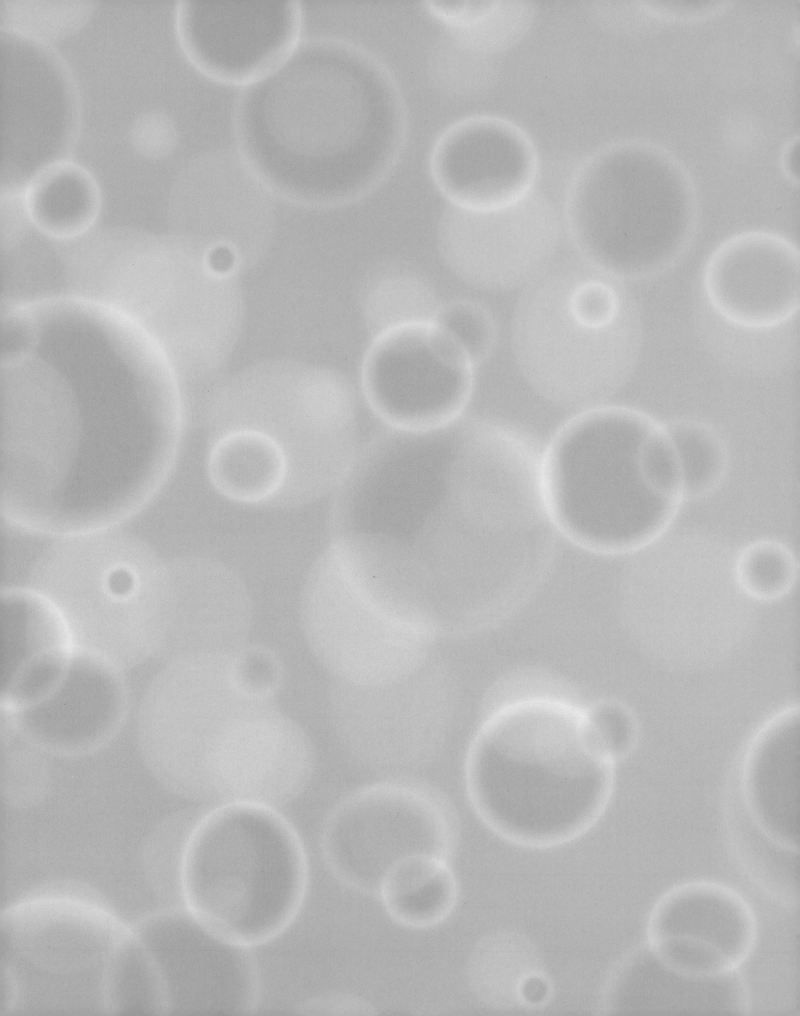

A teacher at Monsters, Incorporated was repeating the rules to her pupils: never scream, and NEVER leave a child's cupboard door open. Why?

"It could let in a child!" bellowed Mr Waternoose, the boss of Monsters, Inc.

The Scarers-in-Training gasped. They knew that children's screams powered Monstropolis. But letting a child into the world of monsters would be deadly to everyone!

Meanwhile, across town, James P. Sullivan was training. His assistant (and best friend), Mike Wazowski, was coaching him. Sulley was a professional Scarer and he needed to keep in top shape.

"Feel the burn," Mike urged. "You call yourself a monster?!"

At Monsters, Inc., Sulley was famous for collecting the most screams.

That was important because the city was having an energy shortage. Human kids were getting harder to scare and Monstropolis needed all the screams it could get.

In the locker room, a monster named Randall popped out at Mike. "AHHH!" Mike shrieked. Randall was creepy and mean … and very jealous of Sulley. Randall would do anything to be the top Scarer.

On the Scare Floor, a giant conveyor belt dropped a child's cupboard door into each station. When the doors were activated, they provided direct links into the bedrooms of children all over the world. Those children's screams would be collected in special canisters.

It was time for the workday to begin. All the Scarers
walked out onto the Scare Floor – these were the best scream
collectors in the business. Each Scarer would walk through
their door – into the room of a sleeping child.

Hopefully, the child would let out a good scream!

After work, Mike rushed to meet his girlfriend, Celia. But Roz blocked his way. "I'm sure you filed your paperwork," rasped the cranky file clerk.

Mike had forgotten! Now he'd miss his date with Celia! Luckily, Sulley offered to finish the paperwork for him.

As he sorted the paperwork, Sulley noticed that someone had left a door on the Scare Floor and its red light was still on. Puzzled, Sulley peeked through the door. Then something grabbed his tail. It was a … CHILD!

Suddenly, Randall appeared on the Scare Floor. Sulley dropped the kid into a soft bag to keep her hidden. Randall pushed a button and sent the child's door back to storage. What would Sulley do now?

Mike and Celia were enjoying a romantic date. Suddenly, Mike spotted Sulley outside the window.

Sulley quickly explained about the child. Mike was horrified … especially when Sulley showed him the girl!

When the CDA (Child Detection Agency) arrived, Mike and Sulley hid the girl in a box and ran. They were in big trouble!

Back at home, Sulley and Mike tried not to let the child touch them.

Then Mike accidentally fell and the little girl started to giggle. Strangely, her laughter made the lights burn brighter!

When Sulley put the child to bed, she was afraid that Randall was in the cupboard. So Sulley stayed until she fell asleep.

"This might sound crazy," Sulley told Mike later, "but I don't think that kid is dangerous."

The next morning, Mike
and Sulley disguised the girl
and took her to work. They
needed to put her back in
her room.

In the locker room, Sulley
and the child played
hide-and-seek. "Boo!" she
said playfully.

Sulley was starting to
really like her. But then they
overheard Randall tell his
assistant that he planned to
"take care of the kid".

Sulley needed to get the
little girl home quickly!

Mike tried to find the right door, but he made a mistake.
"This isn't Boo's door," Sulley exclaimed.

"Boo?!" Mike couldn't believe Sulley had named the child.
And Boo had a nickname for Sulley, too: "Kitty".

Meanwhile, Boo wandered off!

Mike and Sulley split up to find Boo, and Randall cornered
Mike. The nasty monster knew all about Boo. He told Mike to
bring her to the Scare Floor. He said he'd have her door ready....

After they found Boo, Mike and Sulley took her to the Scare Floor, where a door was waiting. But Sulley was still worried.

To prove the open door was safe, Mike went right through – and was grabbed by Randall!

Staying hidden, Sulley and Boo followed the mean monster and discovered that he had invented a cruel new machine. He planned to capture children, then use the machine to extract their screams – and he was about to try the machine out on Mike!

Sulley rescued Mike just in time and they raced towards the training room. He needed to warn the boss, Mr Waternoose, about Randall.

In the training room, Boo accidentally saw Sulley looking scary. Sulley felt awful. For the first time, he realized how mean it was to scare a child.

Mr Waternoose promised to fix everything, but he was really working with Randall!

Mr Waternoose pushed Sulley and Mike through a door into the human world. They were banished to the Himalayan mountains!

Sulley had to get back and help Boo! He found a wardrobe door in a Himalayan village that led him home.

Then he rushed to Randall's secret lab and destroyed the new machine.

As Sulley raced away with Boo, Mike arrived to help. Celia didn't understand what was happening, so Mike quickly tried to explain!

Mike and Sulley climbed onto the machine that carried doors to the Scare Floor. The power wasn't on, but Mike had an idea. He made a funny face. When Boo laughed, the doors began to move! But to send Boo home, they needed to find her door.

Suddenly, Randall grabbed Boo, but she fought back!

"She's not scared of you anymore," Sulley told Randall.

Working together, they beat Randall once and for all.

But Sulley, Mike and Boo weren't safe yet. Now Mr Waternoose and the CDA were controlling the doors.

While Mike distracted the CDA, Sulley escaped with Boo. Unfortunately, Mr Waternoose saw everything.

"Give me the child!" he yelled, running after Sulley.

But luckily, Mike recorded Mr Waternoose yelling, "I'll kidnap a thousand children before I let this company die!" Now all of Monstropolis knew that he had planned to steal children. He was arrested by the head of the CDA – who turned out to be Roz!

It was time for Boo to go home. Sulley followed her into her room and tucked her into bed. Sulley sadly returned to Monstropolis. Roz ordered the CDA to shred Boo's door, so it couldn't be used for scaring anymore. After that, Sulley became president of Monsters, Inc. And the Scare Floor became a Laugh Floor! Sulley and Mike had discovered that laughter produced more power than screams. Monstropolis was saved.

Sulley still missed Boo, though. He had kept a tiny sliver of her door. Before long, however, Mike surprised his pal.

He'd put Boo's door back together! It was missing just one little piece. Sulley inserted the piece, opened the door and saw…. "Boo?" Sulley whispered. "Kitty!" an excited voice replied. The two friends were reunited at last.

When Mike Wazowski was in first grade, he took a field trip with his class. Mike was the smallest monster at Frighton Elementary – and the least popular.

Mrs Graves, his teacher, told everyone to pair up. Nobody wanted to be Mike's partner. "Well, Michael, looks like it's you and me again," said Mrs Graves as she took Mike's hand.

A tour guide met the class and brought them inside. "Stay close together," he said. "We're entering a very dangerous area. This is where we collect the scream energy to power our whole world." Suddenly, a group of Scarers entered. Mike looked at them in awe. As the Scarers walked over the safety line and

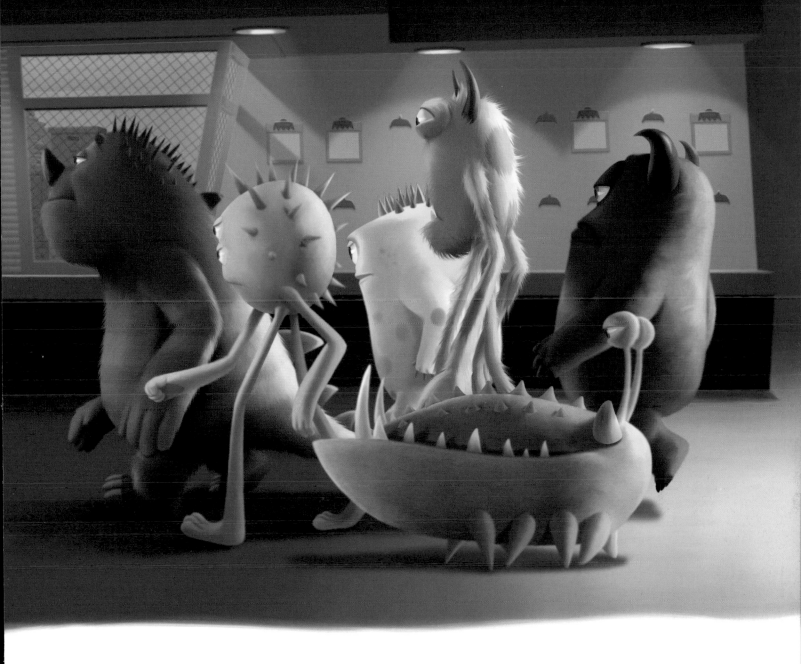

onto a scare floor, the guide warned the kids to stand back.

"Come on, guys! I want to see!" said Mike, as the bigger kids crowded in front of him.

"Out of the way, Wazowski," said a classmate. "You don't belong on a scare floor."

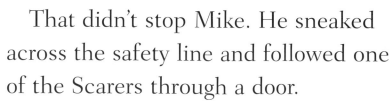

That didn't stop Mike. He sneaked across the safety line and followed one of the Scarers through a door.

Mike watched, amazed, as the Scarer crept up to the sleeping child and frightened him. When Mike emerged from the door, the Scarer told Mike that what he had done was dangerous. But the Scarer was also impressed.

"I didn't even know you were in there," he said with a wink. Suddenly, Mike knew that he wanted to be a Scarer when he grew up.

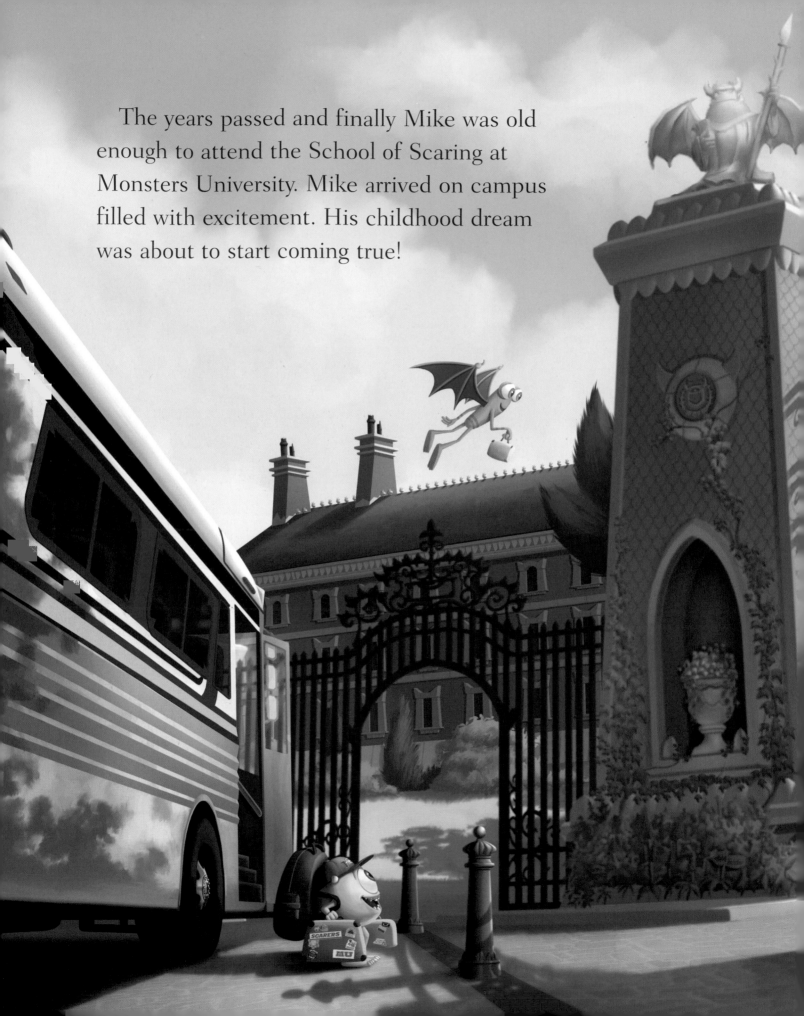

The years passed and finally Mike was old enough to attend the School of Scaring at Monsters University. Mike arrived on campus filled with excitement. His childhood dream was about to start coming true!

One of Mike's classmates was a huge monster named Sulley. He wanted to join the Roar Omega Roar fraternity. Sulley and the RORs made fun of Mike. They thought he was too small and funny looking to be a Scarer.

Mike was determined to study hard and ace his final exam. Meanwhile, all Sulley did was mess around. He thought that being big and having a loud roar were enough to make him the best Scarer.

During the final exam, Mike and Sulley got into a roaring face-off. They accidentally broke Dean Hardscrabble's prized scream canister. She decided that neither of them would be staying in the Scaring Programme and Sulley was kicked out of ROR!

Winning the annual Scare Games was Mike and Sulley's only way of getting back into the Scaring Programme. To compete in the games, they had to join a fraternity. Their only option was to join the least scary group on campus: Oozma Kappa. The members of OK were Don, Squishy, Art and Terri and Terry.

Mike wasn't happy about working with Sulley – but he had no choice.

The first Scare Games event was the Toxicity Challenge. The teams had to get from one end of a sewer tunnel to the other while avoiding stinging glow urchins. As soon as the race started, Mike and Sulley took off and left the rest of the OKs behind. The entire team ended up coming in last. Oozma Kappa was out!

Then, suddenly, one of the winning teams was disqualified for cheating. The OKs were back in!

The next day, the OKs showed Mike some of their talents, but Mike already had a plan. "From now on we are of one mind … my mind," he said.

Sulley rolled his eyes. "You tell them what to do, but not me. Later coach," he muttered, walking away.

The second event, Avoid the Parent, took place in the library. The teams had to capture their flag without getting caught by the librarian! Even though Sulley was no help to the team at all, the OKs managed to take fourth place. Squishy had grabbed the flag and made it out of the library without anyone noticing!

Just as the OKs were starting to feel confident, the RORs made fun of them. They told the OKs they'd never be real Scarers.

Mike decided to take everyone to Monsters, Inc. They sneaked up onto the roof and looked down onto a scare floor. They saw that Scarers came in all shapes and sizes. Everyone was inspired.

Mike and Sulley both admitted that they had been behaving badly. They agreed they needed to start working together.

The following morning, Mike and Sulley bounded out of bed. They couldn't wait to begin training for the next Scare Games event! They packed up their gear, met up with the other OKs and headed off to campus.

Mike worked on getting the team in tip-top shape.
He taught them how to sneak into a bedroom, how
to drop to the floor and how to dodge teenagers.
In between drills, Mike got them to run on
the spot and practise their "scary feet".

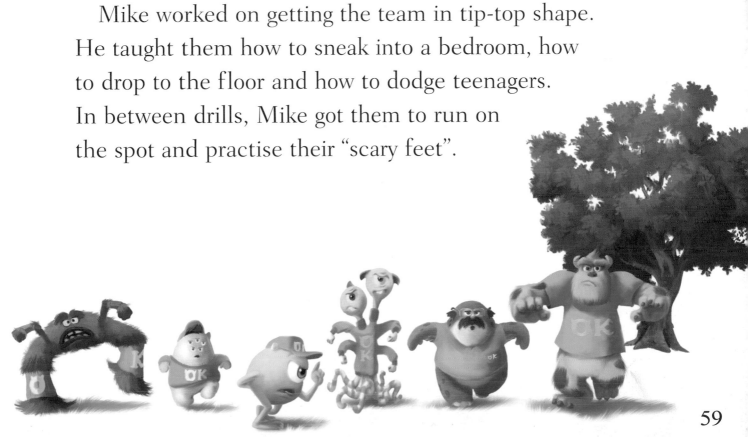

The Oozma Kappas' training paid off. They passed the Don't Scare the Teen event and moved to the next round! Mike helped them to practise for the Hide and Sneak event. The OKs were so well prepared, they came in second.

They were heading to the finals!

Later, Sulley ran into Dean Hardscrabble.

"Tomorrow each of you must prove that you are undeniably scary and I know one of you is not," she said.

Sulley knew that she meant Mike. He didn't want to believe her, but he couldn't help but wonder if she was right.

The RORs and the OKs were going head-to-head in the final Scare Games event. Each competitor had to perform a scare in a simulator.

Mike was the last member of the OKs to perform his scare. He entered the room, sneaked up to the bed, leaped up and roared! The robot child sat bolt upright and screamed.

Mike's scare had given the OKs the highest score. They had won the Scare Games! Don, Squishy, Art, Terri and Terry and Sulley all surrounded Mike and lifted him onto their shoulders. The entire amphitheatre burst into cheers and applause.

"We're in the Scaring Programme!" Sulley cried.

But the moment didn't last long. Mike soon discovered that
Sulley had rigged the controls on the simulator. Mike's difficulty
level had been switched to "easy". He couldn't believe it!

"Well, what was I supposed to do?" Sulley blurted out.
"Let the whole team fail because you don't have it?"

Mike was angry. He stormed off and stole a key to the Door Tech Lab, where students learned how to build doors to the human world. He put a scream canister in place, powered up a door – and opened it! Alarms went off all over campus, sending Hardscrabble and her security guards racing to the lab.

Mike found himself in the wardrobe of a child's room.
He crept out towards the sleeping child and … ROARED!

The youngster sat up and smiled. "You look funny," she said.

Mike couldn't believe it. Suddenly, he realized he wasn't in a child's bedroom. He turned to look and saw that he was in a cabin full of kids!

Meanwhile, Sulley
rushed to the lab. He ran through
the door to rescue Mike and found him in the camp grounds.
"I thought I could show everybody that Mike Wazowski is
something special. But I'm just not," said Mike.
Sulley told Mike he wasn't much different. He had messed
things up his entire life. "I'll never know how you feel, but
you're not the only 'failure' here," he said.

Mike and Sulley discovered that the door back
to the lab had been powered down. They were
trapped! A group of adults was quickly approaching.
"We need to generate enough screams to power
the door from this side," said Mike. As the adults
entered the cabin, Mike signalled to Sulley, who
loomed over the adults and ROARED!

The adults screamed and ran for their lives.
Back in the Door Tech Lab, the door's scream
canister filled to the brim! Hardscrabble
watched in disbelief as the door exploded and
Mike and Sulley blasted into the room.

They had performed an epic scare – but they still got expelled for breaking university rules. Mike and Sulley wondered about their plans for the future. Then Mike had an idea. "There's still one way we could work at a scare floor," he said.

They both got jobs in the Monsters, Inc. mailroom! Mike knew that if they worked hard enough, anything was possible.

This was just the beginning for Team Wazowski and Sullivan.

Mike and Sulley quickly moved up the ranks of the company. They were promoted to cleaners, then to scream canister wranglers and eventually became the first scare team at Monsters, Inc.! On their first day as a team, Mike gazed out at the bustling scare floor.

"You coming, coach?" asked Sulley.

"You better believe it!" Mike replied. He stepped over the red safety line with a huge grin on his face. He was finally where he had always known he belonged.

Marlin was a clownfish, but that didn't mean he had to find life funny.

Marlin had lost his wife and more than four hundred eggs in a ruthless barracuda attack. Only one baby had survived, but he had one damaged fin.

"I promise I will never let anything happen to you … Nemo," Marlin said.

When Nemo was a baby, Marlin wouldn't let him out of his sight. Marlin was so protective, he didn't even like him going beyond their sea anemone home. But, on Nemo's first day of school, Nemo was ready for adventure!

"Wake up, wake up! C'mon!" Nemo exclaimed, swimming circles around his sleeping father.

Before they set off for school, Marlin asked sternly, "What's the one thing we have to remember about the ocean?"

"It's not safe," Nemo sighed.

Nemo met up with his class. The teacher, Mr Ray, assured Marlin that Nemo would be safe. Then Marlin found out they were going to the Drop-off – the very cliff where the barracuda had attacked his family!

At the Drop-off, Nemo wandered off with his new friends, Tad, Sheldon and Pearl. They dared each other to swim up to a dive boat and touch it.

Just then, Marlin
showed up. "You think
you can just do these
things, but you can't!" he
declared. Nemo wanted
to prove his dad wrong.
He swam to the boat
and hit it with his fin.
Marlin scolded Nemo and
told him to swim back
immediately. But suddenly
a diver closed in!

"Daddy! Help me!" Nemo
screamed as he caught sight
 of his reflection in the
diver's mask.

In a flash, the diver had scooped Nemo up in a net. Marlin raced to the surface as the divers sped away. Their boat had sped off so quickly that a diver's mask had fallen overboard.

Marlin rushed to a busy underwater road to get help. "Has anybody seen a boat?" he cried. A beautiful blue tang named Dory told him that she had seen a boat! "Follow me!" she said. However, Dory had a very bad memory. One minute later, she couldn't even remember why Marlin was following her! "Will you quit it?" she asked.

Confused, Marlin turned to swim away. Only to come face to face with …

… a great white shark! He was called Bruce and he was trying to be a vegetarian. He befriended Dory and Marlin and wanted them to meet his like-minded buddies, so they could prove their motto: "Fish are friends, not food!" Dory, who was as enthusiastic as she was forgetful, thought it was a wonderful idea. Terrified Marlin did not.

The sharks held their meetings in a wrecked submarine, surrounded by old sea mines.

"It has been three weeks since my last fish," Bruce told his friends proudly.

Always eager, Dory joined in. "I don't think I've ever eaten a fish."

Just then, Marlin spotted the diver's mask and there was something written on it! It might lead them to Nemo! Dory wanted to show it to the sharks but Marlin didn't.

As they tussled, Dory bumped her nose and it bled a little. Bruce got a sudden craving for a fish dinner!

As Dory and Marlin tried to escape, a mine exploded!

Meanwhile, Nemo found himself in a dentist's fish tank in Sydney, Australia. He soon discovered how small the tank was when he crashed into the side.

A group of fish came out of hiding. Bubbles, Peach, Jacques, Bloat, Deb and Gurgle were thrilled to meet a fish from the open sea.

Later, Nemo learned that he was to be a present for the dentist's niece, Darla.

"She's a fish-killer," whispered Peach.

That night, a ceremony was held to make Nemo an official member of their group. All Nemo had to do was swim through the RING OF FIRE!

It sounded scary, but it was really just a stream of bubbles. Nemo bravely swam through the bubbles and into the gang's hearts.

Afterwards Gill, the leader of the tank announced, "From this moment on, you will be known as 'Shark Bait'." Next, he revealed his plan to escape from the tank....

Back in the ocean, Dory had dropped the mask into a deep trench! She and Marlin swam after it, right into an anglerfish.

Suddenly, Dory remembered she could read!

"P. Sherman, 42 Wallaby Way, Sydney," said Dory.

Thinking quickly, Marlin trapped the anglerfish inside the mask so they could escape. The pair were so excited – they knew where to find Nemo!

Marlin told Dory he was going to Sydney alone.
"You mean you don't like me?" Dory asked.

A school of moonfish rushed over and were
angry with Marlin for upsetting Dory. They
refused to help Marlin but, when
he turned his back, they told
Dory how to get to Sydney.
"Follow the East Australian
Current," they said.

Then, they gave her a
warning. "When you come
to a trench, swim through it,
not over it."

When they finally got to the trench, however, Marlin insisted that swimming over it would be much safer. Soon they were surrounded by stinging jellyfish! Dory thought it was fun to bounce on top of them! They had found a safe way through – but they were tired and had been stung by the jellyfish. They needed help.

Some sea turtles rescued Marlin and Dory. Their run-in with the jellyfish had left them in bad shape.

"Takin' on the jellies – awesome!" exclaimed Crush, a surfer turtle.

Marlin watched as Crush encouraged his children to be adventurous. Crush thought it taught them important lessons. Watching Crush's kids made Marlin wonder if he had been too protective of Nemo.

Tales of Marlin's adventures were spreading far and wide.

Nigel, a friendly pelican who knew the tank gang, eventually heard the stories and rushed to tell Nemo the incredible news.

Nemo was amazed. He had always thought his dad was a bit of a scaredy-fish. The thought that he was battling his way to Sydney filled the little fish with pride.

Nemo was inspired by his dad's bravery and he was determined to escape. To his friends' horror, Nemo darted into the filter and successfully jammed it! Everyone cheered!

Very soon, the tank gang was swimming in slimy, green water. They couldn't have been happier! Dr Sherman was going to have to clean the tank before Darla arrived!

Back in the ocean, Marlin and Dory said goodbye to the turtles, but soon found themselves swallowed up inside the mouth of a massive whale.

"It's okay, I speak Whale," Dory assured Marlin. "He either said we should move to the back of his throat, or he wants a root beer float," she translated.

It turned out the whale was only giving the two brave little fish a lift. They were soon squirted out of the whale's blowhole, right into Sydney Harbour!

They nearly ended up as breakfast for hungry seagulls, but luckily, Nigel rushed to their rescue.

"Hop inside my mouth if you want to live," he whispered.

Nigel snatched them up, filled his beak with some water and took off. The hungry seagulls followed, but Nigel played a trick on them and the seagulls flew right into a boat's sail!

Meanwhile, the dentist had cleaned the tank water with a fancy new automated cleaner – while the fish were still in the tank!

The escape plan was ruined.

Nemo was lifted out of the tank and plopped into a bag. Darla had arrived. Nemo had one last chance – he played dead, hoping that he would get flushed down the toilet and out into the ocean.

Nigel stumbled through the window with Marlin and Dory and saw Nemo floating upside down in the plastic bag. The dentist quickly shooed Nigel away, but in the commotion he dropped Nemo. The bag burst open. "I get a fishy!" squealed Darla as she reached out to grab him.

Gill flipped himself onto the tray beside Nemo.
"Tell your dad I said 'hi'," he said. Then Gill smacked
his tail on a dental mirror, catapulting Nemo over
Darla's waiting hands and into the spit sink. The little
fish escaped down the drain!

Back in the harbour, Nigel dropped Dory and Marlin into the sea. Marlin was heartbroken. He thought that he had lost Nemo for good and swam off to be on his own.

Nemo soon met Dory. At first, she had no memory of who he was ... but when she finally did remember, Dory knew she had to reunite Nemo with his dad straight away!

Together, they swam after Marlin as fast as Nemo's little fins would let them.

There was a happy reunion between Marlin and
Nemo. Marlin finally realized that even though
Nemo was a little fish, he was capable of doing very
big things! They had both learned that life was an
adventure to be lived to the full.

Meanwhile, the tank gang had finally managed to break the new filter, forcing Dr Sherman to clean the tank. They had made their daring escape and were now floating in Sydney Harbour! Only one problem remained: how would they get out of those bags?

Andy was a young boy with a big imagination. He loved playing with all his toys, but his favourite was Sheriff Woody, a pull-string cowboy doll. Andy spent hours playing with Woody – together, they fought bad guys, rescued good guys and had all kinds of exciting adventures. Andy took Woody everywhere.

Woody lived in Andy's bedroom with Slinky Dog, Rex
the dinosaur, Mr Potato Head, Hamm the pig, Bo Peep
and all the other toys. These toys were special. When no
onc was around, they came to life! One by one, all the
toys peeked out of the cupboard, from beneath the bed,
and out of the toy chest.

Woody called all the toys together. "Andy and his family are moving to a new house soon," he told them. "That's why Andy's having his birthday party today."

The toys were worried. A birthday party meant new toys. What if Andy liked his new toys more than he liked them? "One of us might be replaced!" groaned Rex.

"There's no need to worry," Woody promised. "Andy wouldn't do that."

"They're here!" Hamm shouted suddenly. Looking out of the window, he had spotted Andy's guests starting to arrive.

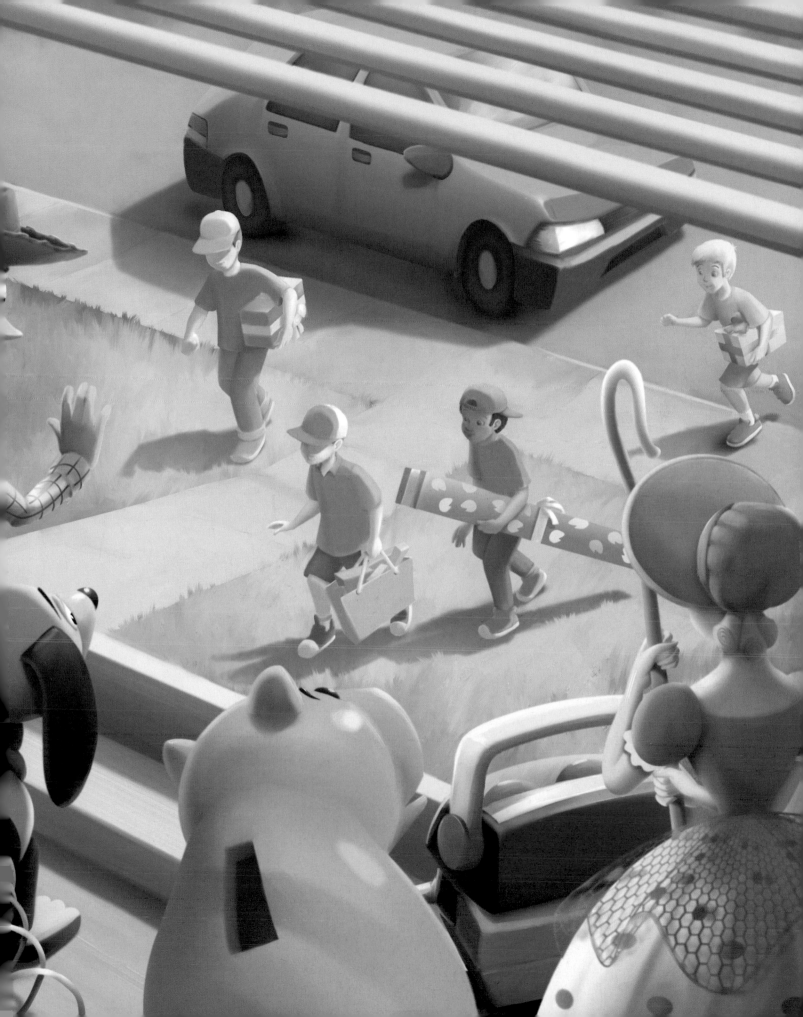

"Sergeant, establish a recon post downstairs. Code red!"
Woody sent the Green Army Men downstairs to spy on Andy's
party. Using a jump rope, the soldiers scrambled down to the first
floor, then set up a baby monitor inside a potted plant. Hidden,
the soldiers broadcast descriptions of the presents as they were
unwrapped, sending the news back to Andy's room. Luckily,
nothing sounded too threatening … until the last package. All the
kids gasped as they saw…. Just then, the baby monitor cut out.
The toys were frantic! What was that last present?

Andy brought him up to the bedroom and left him there. "I'm Buzz Lightyear, space ranger," the newcomer said. The new toy claimed to be a space hero who had just landed on Earth. He also claimed he could fly. Then he tried to prove it, by bouncing off a ball and shouting, "To infinity and beyond!" The other toys were impressed, but Woody rolled his eyes.

"That's just falling with style," he complained. Everyone thought Buzz was wonderful. Everyone, that is, except Woody. Woody was jealous! "You're NOT a space ranger," he sneered. "You're just a toy like the rest of us!"

Suddenly, they heard barking outside and rushed to the window. Sid, the boy next door, was attacking a toy soldier. His dog, Scud, was watching excitedly.

"Sid's horrible," Rex told Buzz. "He tortures toys just for fun."

The toys watched helplessly as Sid destroyed the soldier.

As the toys went back to their places, Woody was still mad with Buzz. He thought that if he aimed the remote control car at Buzz, the new toy would fall behind the desk and Andy wouldn't be able to find him. But the car sped out of control, and everything went wrong – ending up with Buzz falling out of the window. All the toys rushed to the window to see where Buzz had fallen.

"It was an accident!" said Woody. But none of the toys would believe him.

Suddenly, Andy burst into the room. He was going to Pizza Planet and wanted to take a toy.

"I can't find Buzz, Mum," he called. "I'll have to take Woody instead."

But Buzz did go with them! He had fallen into a bush and leaped onto the car just as it drove away.

Pizza Planet was full of arcade games. Buzz thought one
was a spaceship and crawled inside, followed by Woody.

It was crammed with toy aliens that were picked up by a
claw. Woody and Buzz were horrified when they saw who had
managed to grab them – it was Sid, Andy's cruel neighbour.

Back in Sid's bedroom, Woody and Buzz were terrified.
They were surrounded by weird-looking mutants that Sid had made
from toys he had broken. The mutants crawled closer and closer
towards Woody and Buzz. "Get back, you savages!" cried Woody.
"Buzz, come on, we've got to get out of here – fast!"

They had just escaped,
when Buzz heard a voice calling:

"Come in, Buzz Lightyear, this is Star Command."

Buzz left Woody hiding in a cupboard and ran towards the voice.
But it was only a television advertisement for the Buzz Lightyear toy.
Buzz was stunned. "Is it true?" he whispered. "Am I really ... a toy?"
Desperate to prove he was a real space ranger, Buzz tried to fly.
But he crashed to the floor, breaking his arm.

NOT A FLYING TOY

Woody found Buzz and took him back to Sid's room. Looking out of Sid's window, he saw his old friends in Andy's room.

"Hey guys, help!" Woody called to them, waving madly.

But the toys were angry with Woody because they thought he had hurt Buzz.

"Murderer!" shouted Mr Potato Head, as Slinky Dog pulled down the blind.

Woody turned sadly away from the window – it seemed that he and Buzz were prisoners in Sid's house.

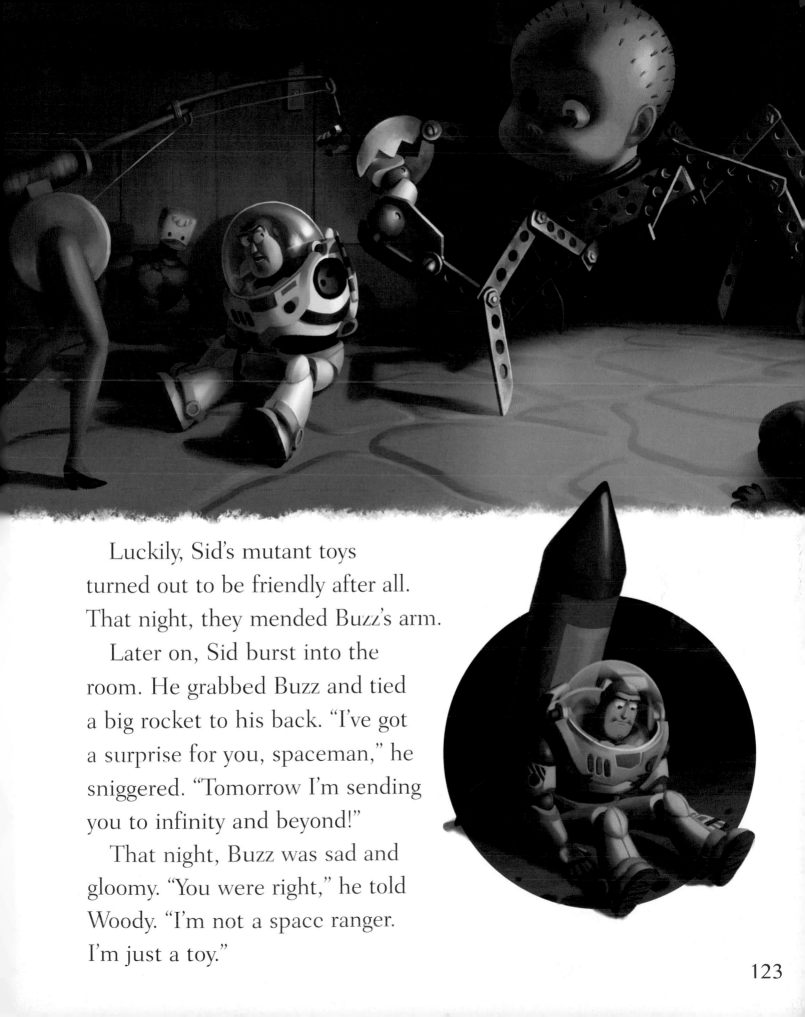

Luckily, Sid's mutant toys turned out to be friendly after all. That night, they mended Buzz's arm.

Later on, Sid burst into the room. He grabbed Buzz and tied a big rocket to his back. "I've got a surprise for you, spaceman," he sniggered. "Tomorrow I'm sending you to infinity and beyond!"

That night, Buzz was sad and gloomy. "You were right," he told Woody. "I'm not a space ranger. I'm just a toy."

123

"But being a toy is what makes you special," said Woody. "You're Andy's toy and he thinks you're great. He needs us, and we have to get back to him!" Buzz thought for a moment.

"You're right," he said at last. "Let's go!"

But it was too late! Sid's alarm clock rang out.

Brrrrring

Sid reached out, smashed the clock and picked up Buzz.

"Today's the day, spaceman," he said. He rushed downstairs and into the garden, where he started to build a launch pad....

Woody turned to Sid's toys for help.

"Please help me save Buzz," he begged them. "He's my friend."

The mutant toys smiled at Woody and nodded. Together, they worked out a plan to rescue Buzz.

Out in the garden, Sid was ready to light the fuse on Buzz's rocket. "Ten! Nine! Eight ..." he counted.

10, 9, 8, 7, 6, 5, 4, 3, 2 ....

Suddenly, Sid spied Woody on the ground. As he picked up the cowboy, his other toys crawled out and surrounded him. Then Woody spoke....

"Aaaaah!" yelled Sid. "Help! These toys are alive!" Screaming, he ran into the house.

Woody and Buzz were free! They thanked the mutant toys for their help and began to make their way home. But Andy's family were just driving away, followed by the removal van!

"It's moving day!" gasped Buzz.

"There they go!" yelled Woody. "Quick! We've got to catch them!"

The two friends rushed after the van. Buzz managed to climb onto the van's back bumper. But Woody was caught by Scud, who had chased them.

"Get away!" shouted Woody, trying to free himself. Scud growled louder....

Bravely, Buzz leaped off the bumper and fought off Scud, who ran back to his house. Now Woody was on the van – but Buzz was stranded on the road!

Woody yanked open the back of the van and rummaged through the boxes until he found RC Car. Using the remote control, Woody sent RC back to pick up Buzz. But Andy's toys didn't understand what Woody was doing, and angrily threw him off the van! Luckily, Buzz and RC picked up Woody as they came speeding back. Finally realizing what had really happened, the other toys tried to help ...

... but RC's batteries ran out. Woody watched, heartbroken, as the moving van chugged further and further away. Then they realized – Buzz still had the rocket on his back!

Once the fuse was lit, Woody whooped with excitement. As they rose upward, Woody let go of RC, who landed in the van. Buzz and Woody whooshed into the sky. Just as the rocket was about to explode, Buzz snapped open his space wings and broke free.

"Buzz, you're flying!" Woody exclaimed.

"This isn't flying," Buzz replied. "This is falling with style!"

Buzz and Woody soared through the sky, then glided down towards Andy's car. While Andy was looking out of the window, the two dropped unnoticed through the car's open sunroof, landing safely on the back seat.

Hearing a thump, Andy looked over. "Woody! Buzz!" he shouted. He hugged them close, thrilled to have his two favourite toys back. Woody and Buzz had made it home.

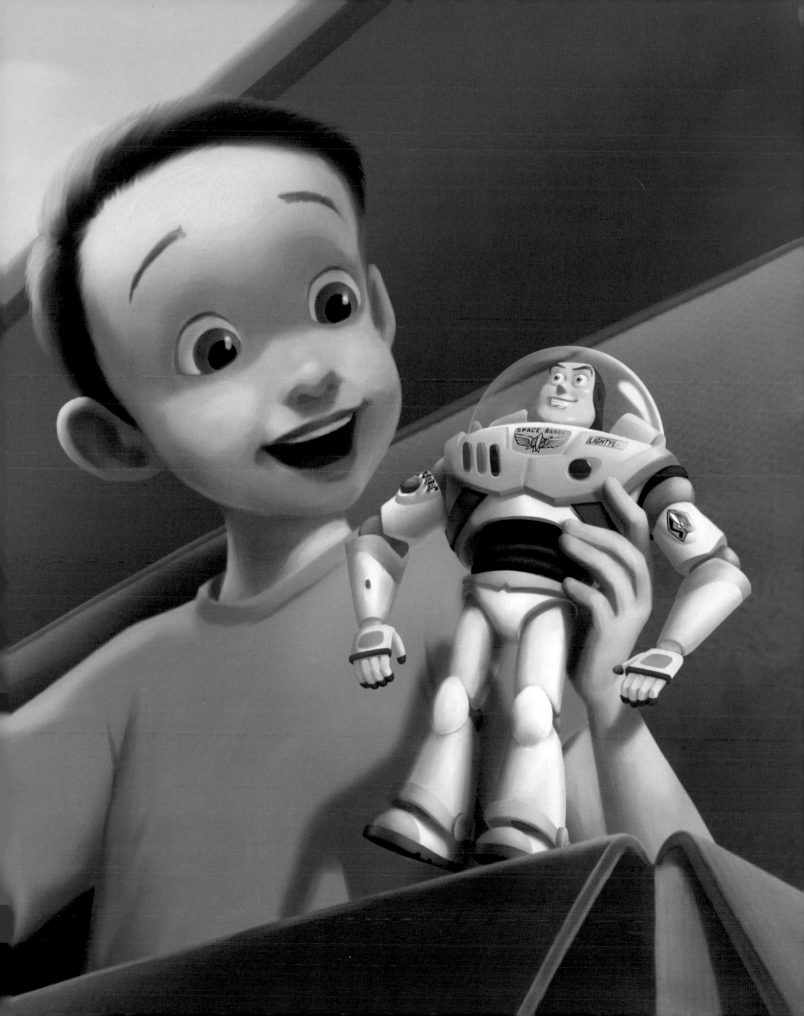

Everyone settled happily into the new house. But all too soon, it was Christmas – which meant new toys.

"You aren't worried, are you?" Woody asked Buzz, as they sat listening to the baby monitor. "What could Andy possibly get that is worse than you?" Woody teased. They listened intently as Andy unwrapped his first present ... and suddenly Buzz and Woody's eyes widened, as they heard an unmistakable sound: woof-woof!

"Wow! A puppy!" Andy cried.

"Hey, Woody! Ready to go to Cowboy Camp?" Andy shouted, bursting into the bedroom. Woody was very excited. With a few spare minutes before leaving for camp, Andy grabbed Woody and Buzz, his two favourites, for a quick adventure. "Never tangle with the unstoppable duo of Woody and Buzz Lightyear!" he proclaimed, linking the toys' arms together. Suddenly, there was a loud RIIIPPPP!

Woody's shoulder had ripped open! Andy's mum suggested fixing Woody on the way to camp, but Andy shook his head and sighed. "No, just leave him."

"I'm sorry," his mum replied. "But you know toys don't last forever."

Woody sat on the shelf and watched sadly as Andy left without him. And he didn't feel any better when he found Wheezy, a toy penguin, who'd been sitting broken and forgotten on the shelf for months. Was that Woody's future, too?

Suddenly, the toys spotted something truly terrifying – Andy's mum was putting up a sign outside: YARD SALE! She chose Wheezy as one of the sale items. Thinking quickly, Woody waited till Andy's mum was out of sight, then whistled for Buster, Andy's friendly puppy. Together, they sneaked outside, grabbed Wheezy and headed back to safety. But because his arm was injured, Woody lost his grip and tumbled to the ground. Then, a strange man noticed Woody, picked him up ...

... and stole him! From the upstairs window, the other toys watched in horror as the man tossed Woody into the trunk of his car. Buzz couldn't let Woody be taken away so easily, so he jumped out of the window and slid down the drainpipe, racing to rescue his friend.

But he was too late. All Buzz saw was a licence plate, LZT YBRN, and a few feathers floating in the air, as the car sped away.

The strange man took
Woody to his apartment
and put him in a glass case.
Once he was alone, Woody
ran to the door, trying to
escape. But it was no use.
He was trapped. POP!
A packing box suddenly
burst open and Woody
was knocked off his feet
by a galloping toy horse.

"Yee-haw! It's really you!"
shouted a cowgirl, squeezing
Woody in a big hug. The
cowgirl said her name
was Jessie and the horse
was Bullseye. Then she
introduced the Prospector.
All of them were thrilled to
see Woody.

Meanwhile, back in Andy's room, Buzz and the other toys held an urgent meeting. They were trying to solve the big mystery: who took Woody? Buzz gathered up the clues – the licence plate, the chicken feather – and finally figured out that the man must be from Al's Toy Barn, a toy store that advertised on TV. In fact, he had to be Al, the goofy salesman who dressed in a chicken suit!

But now that they knew who the culprit was,
what could the toys do?

"Woody once risked his life to save me," Buzz
told the others. "I couldn't call myself his friend if
I weren't willing to do the same."

Buzz decided to lead a rescue party to the toy store,
to see if they could find Woody. Together, with a little
help from Slinky, they jumped off the roof. "To Al's
Toy Barn and beyond!" Buzz cried.

At Al's apartment, Woody couldn't
understand how the other toys recognized
him. "How do you know my name?" he asked.
   "Why, you don't know who you are, do you?" the Prospector said.
Bullseye turned on the lights to reveal that the room was filled with
items carrying Woody's picture: posters, magazines, lunchboxes, plates
and toys. Woody couldn't believe his eyes! Then Jessie showed Woody
an old television show, Woody's Roundup. Woody was the star!

Woody laughed as he, Jessie and Bullseye explored
all the memorabilia from Woody's Roundup – they
blew bubbles, put pennies in a bank and raced
across a spinning record player. "Now it's on to the
museum!" the Prospector exclaimed.

"What museum?" Woody stopped in confusion.
The Prospector explained that they had become
valuable collectibles. Al planned to sell them as a set
to a Japanese museum for a lot of money.

Buzz and his rescue team had almost reached Al's Toy Barn. They just needed to cross one last, very busy street. Luckily, Buzz noticed a pile of orange traffic cones. He told everyone to grab one and then, slowly, they ventured across the street, hiding under the cones. Soon, the street was filled with skidding, honking, crashing cars, all trying to avoid the strange, moving traffic cones. But the toys barely noticed. They'd arrived at Al's Toy Barn.

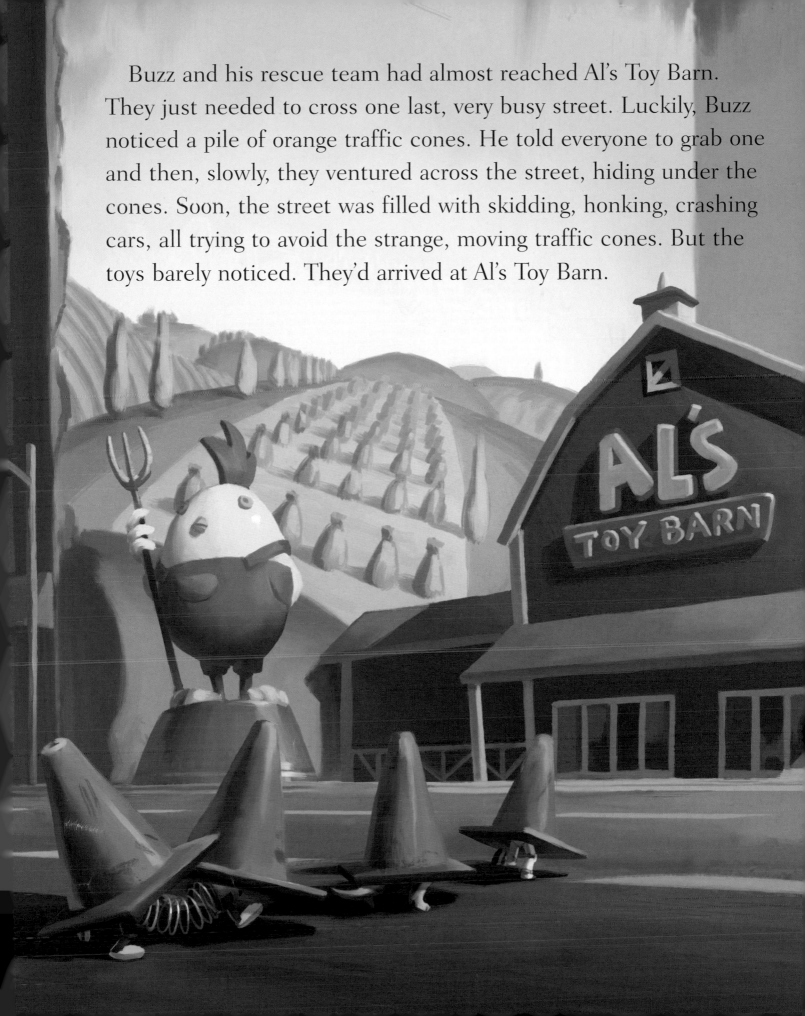

Inside the Toy Barn, Buzz looked up at an amazing display of new Buzz Lightyear toys – each one was wearing a super utility belt.

"I could use that!" thought Buzz.

WHAP! His hand was clenched by a new Buzz space ranger. And, before long, Andy's toy was overpowered and imprisoned inside a box on the shelf.

Then New Buzz ran to join Andy's toys – and not one of them realized they'd left the real Buzz behind.

Buzz struggled free from his box just in time to see his friends head out of the front door, inside Al's bag! Racing to catch up, he crashed – SMACK! – into the automatic doors.

To make the doors re-open, Buzz knocked a nearby pile of toy boxes onto the sensor mat. One box remained stuck between the doors. Opening and closing, the doors hit the box again and again. At last, it popped open, and a dark figure rose up. It was the evil Emperor Zurg!

He watched Buzz running away from the Toy Barn and growled, "Destroy Buzz Lightyear!"

The toys hitched a ride back to Al's apartment block, hidden in his bag. They snuck through the vents and finally arrived at his apartment.

They charged into the room. New Buzz grabbed Woody and ran. Everything became even more confusing when the real Buzz showed up, too!

"There's no time to explain," Andy's Buzz said, "Woody, you're in danger here." He knew that Al wanted to send Woody to Japan.

But Woody didn't want to leave. He worried that Andy would not want him any more, so he stayed in the apartment and watched his friends leave.

Soon, though, Woody realized Buzz was right – he belonged with Andy. "Hey, Buzz! Wait!" he shouted as he ran towards the vent to follow them.

But the Prospector blocked Woody's path! After a lifetime in his box, he was determined to go to the museum.

"And no hand-me-down cowboy doll is gonna mess it up for me now!" he shouted.

Suddenly, they heard footsteps – Al was coming!

Al packed Woody and the Roundup gang into a case, and dashed out of the door.

"Quick! To the lift!" Buzz shouted, hoping to catch up. But on the roof of the lift, Emperor Zurg blocked their path – he had followed Buzz all the way from the Toy Barn!

As Zurg battled with Buzz, Rex turned away, terrified – and knocked Zurg off the lift with his tail!

"I did it! I finally defeated Zurg!" Rex cried happily.

Andy's toys said goodbye to the New Buzz and raced through the hall after Woody.

Luckily, Mr Potato Head spotted a pizza truck nearby and the toys jumped in. And so, with Buzz at the steering wheel, Slinky on the pedals, Rex as navigator, and Hamm and Mr Potato Head working the gear-stick, they zigzagged their way to the airport. There, the toys ran inside, desperately looking for Al.

The toys climbed into a pet carrier so they could move around the airport without being seen – Slinky even barked a few times so it would seem like there was a real pet inside!

They found Al, and his green suitcase full of toys, at the check-in desk. He put the case on the conveyor belt and the toys followed … still inside the pet carrier!

"Woody, are you there?" Buzz called, as he opened the catch on Al's suitcase.

POW! The Prospector came out fighting, hitting Buzz hard.

Woody fought back against the Prospector and he and Bullseye managed to escape. But Jessie was still trapped inside the suitcase.

"I'm not letting Jessie down!" Woody thought. "She deserves another chance to play with a kid who loves her."

Woody, Buzz and Bullseye galloped after Jessie towards the plane.

Woody dived into a golf bag just as it was being loaded onto the plane. Then he searched through the bags, until he found Jessie.

"Oh, Woody, I knew you'd come!" she cried.

"We're not out of here yet!" said Woody grimly. "And we haven't got much time left!"

They felt the plane begin to move towards the runway. They crawled through a hatch, down to the plane's wheels.

The plane was already speeding down the runway – Woody and Jessie could barely hold on … then Woody slipped! Jessie caught him just in time, but his arm was starting to rip even more….

Thinking quickly, Woody tried a daring trick. He twirled his pull-string and lassoed a bolt on the wheels. Then he grabbed Jessie's hand and they swung towards the ground. At the same moment, Bullseye and Buzz galloped towards them, catching them as they fell!

Later that day, Andy arrived back from Cowboy Camp. He was delighted to be home. And he was even more pleased to see Bullseye and Jessie with the other toys on his bed! He started to play with them at once. The toys all smiled. They were safe at last – back in Andy's room!

The End

Goodbye!